The Three Little Pigs

The Three Little Pigs

Retold by Jane Resnick
Illustrated by J.L. Macias S.

Once upon a time, there were three little pigs, Pinky, Perky and Percival, who lived by the edge of the forest. One day, they decided they were ready to go out into the world and build their own houses.

Percival was the most serious pig. "I have heard that a wolf lives in this forest," he warned his brothers, "and I am going to build a house that is strong and safe. I don't want any wolf knocking down *my* door."

"Oh, don't be silly," said Pinky, playing his flute and dancing to a merry tune.

"Who's afraid of the big, bad wolf, anyway," said Perky, playing along on his fiddle.

Pinky and Perky just wouldn't listen to Percival's warning. Lazy, and foolish too, they built the easiest houses they could think of. Pinky built a house of straw and Perky made his of sticks and they finished in no time at all.

"Well, what do you think?" Pinky asked Perky.

"Looks good to me," he answered without a second thought.

Then Pinky took his flute and Perky grabbed his fiddle and off they went to play in the forest. "Percival is so silly," snickered Perky. "He keeps telling us not to play in the forest. 'Watch out for the big, bad wolf,' he says, but I don't see any old wolf, do you?" But no sooner had he spoken when the bushes rustled, the leaves shook, and the wolf jumped out right before them!

Pinky reached his house without a moment to spare. The wolf was right behind him. Slamming the door shut, Pinky felt the whole house shake and he began to shake too. Quivering behind the door, he heard the gruff voice of the wolf calling to him.

"Little pig, little pig, let me come in!"

"No," cried Pinky as firmly as he could, "not by the hair of your chinny-chin-chin!"

"Then I'll huff and I'll puff and I'll blow your house in!" shouted the wolf. Pinky was too frightened to reply but the wolf wasn't waiting for an answer. He took a deep breath. He huffed and he puffed and he blew the little straw house to pieces!

"It's the wolf!" Pinky cried as he ran into Perky's house, slamming the door behind him.

"Little pig, little pig, let me come in!" the wolf called impatiently.

"Not by the hair of your chinny-chin-chin," the brothers shouted back together.

"Then I'll huff and I'll puff and I'll blow your house in!" Taking a deep breath, the wolf huffed and he puffed and he blew the little stick house to bits!

Percival was amazed to see his brothers speeding toward his house. "Let us come in! Let us come in!" they shouted, terrified. The two little pigs were so out of breath they could hardly speak. "The wolf's coming and he wants us for lunch!" Perky squealed. "Quick! Get inside!" Percival exclaimed.

Pinky and Perky rushed into the house. Hiding under the bed, they peeked out only to see Percival calmly blocking the door with a big piece of wood.

"Little pig, little pig, let me come in," the wolf called.

"Not by the hair of your chinny-chin-chin," Percival answered proudly.

"Then I'll huff and I'll puff and I'll blow your house in!" he growled. So he huffed and he puffed, and he huffed and he puffed, but he could not blow that house in.

However, the stubborn and hungry wolf did not give up. He jumped onto the roof and began to climb down the chimney. "I'll have my dinner yet," he said to himself gleefully. But the wolf didn't know what Percival had done. That smart little pig had put a huge pot of water in the fireplace and then built a big fire.

Down the chimney the wolf slid, right into the kettle of water just as it began to boil furiously. "Yeeooww!" he screamed when his tail hit the water.

For a moment the three little pigs didn't know whether to be frightened or glad. They had tricked the wolf *and* they were safe! Pinky and Perky were astonished, but Percival wasn't at all surprised. He knew he wasn't going to let that wolf get him ever!

While the three happy pigs were celebrating their victory, the terrified wolf had sprung up the chimney, scrambled off the roof, and had run far, far into the woods—away from those three smart, little pigs.

The wolf had certainly learned his lesson. With his tail on fire and his eyes tearing, he swore he would never chase after little pigs again, especially those living in brick houses!